The Top and the Ball

QUALITY TIME™ CLASSICS

TALES
OF
HANS CHRISTIAN ANDERSEN

The Little Match Girl
The Steadfast Tin Soldier
The Top and the Ball
The Woman with the Eggs

Library of Congress Cataloging-in-Publication Data

Erickson, Jon E.
  The top and the ball.

  (Quality time classics)
  Summary: A Top's love for a proud Ball does not receive the reward for which he hopes, as first his advances are rejected and then the toys are separated for several years.
  [1. Fairy tales. 2. Toys--Fiction] I. Andersen, H. C. (Hans Christian), 1805-1875. Toppen og bolden. II. Mogensen, Jan, ill. III. Title. IV. Series.
  PZ8.E69 1987   [E]   87-42584
  ISBN 1-55532-343-X
  ISBN 1-55532-318-9 (lib. bdg.)

This North American edition first published in 1987 by

Gareth Stevens, Inc.
7221 West Green Tree Road
Milwaukee, Wisconsin 53223, USA

First published as *Toppen og Bolden* with an original copyright by Mallings, Copenhagen.

Typeset by Web Tech, Inc., Milwaukee

2   3   4   5   6   7   8   9   92   91   90   89   88

The Top and the Ball

by Hans Christian Andersen

retold by Jon Erickson

illustrations by Jan Mogensen

Gareth Stevens Publishing
Milwaukee

A Top and a Ball lay together in a toy
drawer. Said the Top to the Ball, "Let's get
married, since we live together here anyway!"

But the Ball, made of fine leather, thought herself too fine a lady to answer such a question.

The next day, the little boy who owned the toys painted the Top red and yellow. Then he hammered a brass nail in the middle of the Top. How handsome the Top looked as he spun around!

"Look! What do you think of me *now*?" said the Top to the Ball. "Shall we get married? What a pair we'd make! You can jump and I can dance. We could be so happy."

"That's what *you* think!" the Ball answered. "Did you know that my mother and father were a pair of the finest slippers ever made, and that inside me I have a cork?"

"Yes, well — *I'm* made of mahogany, and the mayor of the city made me himself!" said the Top.

"Do you expect me to believe that?" asked the Ball.

"May I never spin again if I am lying!" said the Top.

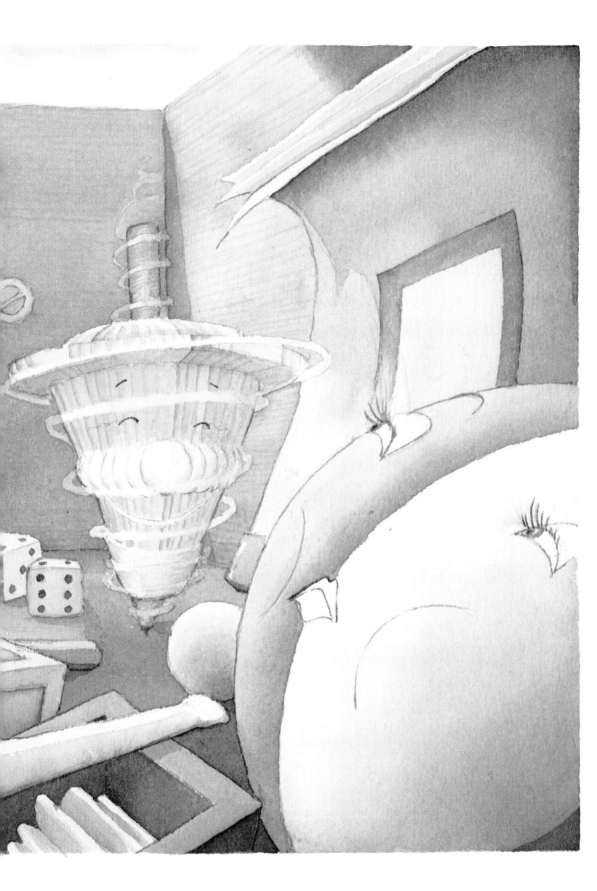

"You speak pretty well for yourself," said the Ball. "But I have to say no. I'm almost engaged to the Swallow, you know. Every time I jump up in the air, he pokes his head out of the nest and says, 'Will you? Will you?' Though I've never said yes, I've *thought* it, and *that's* almost as good as being engaged. But I promise I'll never forget you!"

"A lot of good *that* does me!" the Top moaned, and neither one said a word after that.

The next day the little boy went outside to play with the Ball. The Top watched as she flew higher and higher with each bounce, as if she were trying to find the Swallow. On the ninth bounce the Ball flew high in the air, but she did not come back. The boy searched and searched. But the Ball was gone.

"I know where she is!" sighed the Top. "She's married and living with the Swallow!"

The more the Top thought about the Ball, the more he loved her. Because he couldn't have her, he loved her even more. The Top spun around and around, humming and thinking of nothing but the Ball. She became more and more beautiful in his memory.

Many years passed in this way, until he thought of her only as an old love.

The Top wasn't so young anymore. Then one day he was painted completely gold. He had never looked so good! He leaped and spun for joy. But suddenly he spun wildly — and he disappeared!

Everyone looked and looked. But he was
nowhere to be found.

Where had he gone?

Well, he had spun into a trash bin. Here, he found himself with a lot of dead leaves and rubbish that had fallen from the gutter on the roof.

"What a place to land!" thought the Top. "I'll soon lose my gold paint here. And look at the riff-raff I'm stuck with!"

He glanced sideways at a scraggly cabbage stalk, and then he saw what looked like a rotten old apple. But it wasn't an apple at all. It was an old ball that had been in the rain gutter for years.

"Thank goodness. At last here's someone good enough for me to talk to!" said the Ball, seeing the Top. "You wouldn't know it to see me now, but I was handmade from the finest leather and have a cork inside me. I was about to marry a Swallow when I got stuck up in the gutter on the roof. I was up there for five years and got soaked through. That's a long time for a young lady like me!"

The Top didn't say a thing. But the more he heard, the more sure he was that she was his old love.

Just then the cleaning girl came to clean out the bin.

"Hey look! Here's the gold Top!"

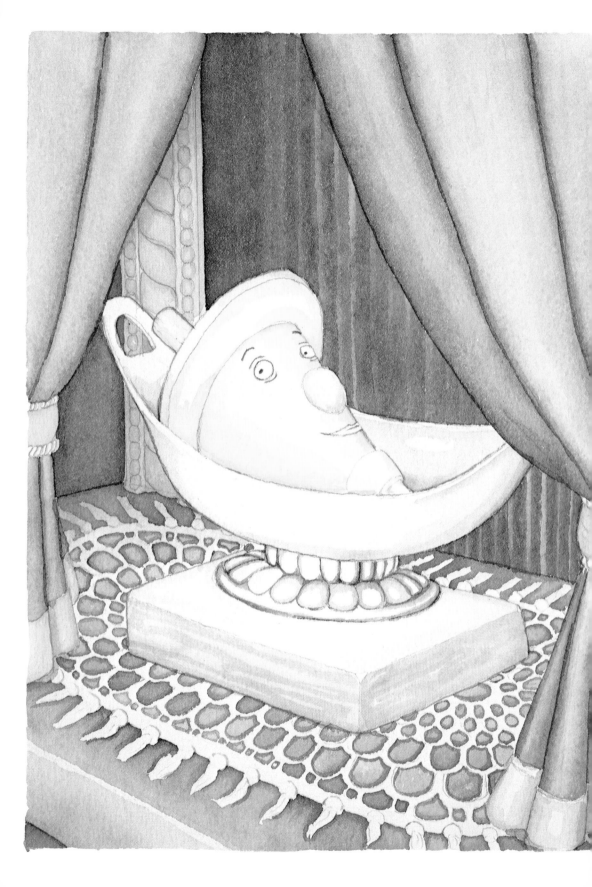

The Top was brought back into the house, where he got lots of attention. Nobody spoke of the Ball at all, and the Top never thought of her again....

When you learn your sweetheart has been soaking in a gutter for five years, love can fade away. You may not even know her when you meet her in a pile of trash!

THE END